Popeye

Meets Beulah

and

She's A Bully

Written by
Betts Heeley Huff

Holland Kinney, Illustrator

AuthorHouse™
1663 Liberty Drive
Bloomington, IN 47403
www.authorhouse.com
Phone: 833-262-8899

Because of the dynamic nature of the Internet, any web addresses or links contained in this
book may have changed since publication and may no longer be valid. The views expressed
in this work are solely those of the author and do not necessarily reflect the views of
the publisher, and the publisher hereby disclaims any responsibility for them.

Any people depicted in stock imagery provided by Getty Images are models,
and such images are being used for illustrative purposes only.
Certain stock imagery © Getty Images.

This book is printed on acid-free paper.

ISBN: 978-1-6655-2720-0 (sc)
ISBN: 978-1-6655-2722-4 (hc)
ISBN: 978-1-6655-2721-7 (e)

Print information available on the last page.

Published by AuthorHouse 06/03/2021

authorHOUSE®

Say 'Hi' to Popeye

The barnyard is a happy place. My visits there are always special. There is plenty of room for us to roam around, dance, skip rope, and just enjoy our friendship.

We all came from other places, even faraway countries. We are different from one another. The colors of our skin. The languages we speak. The foods we eat. The games we play. And we all agree that this is the best place in the world.

Then Beulah arrived!

Help!

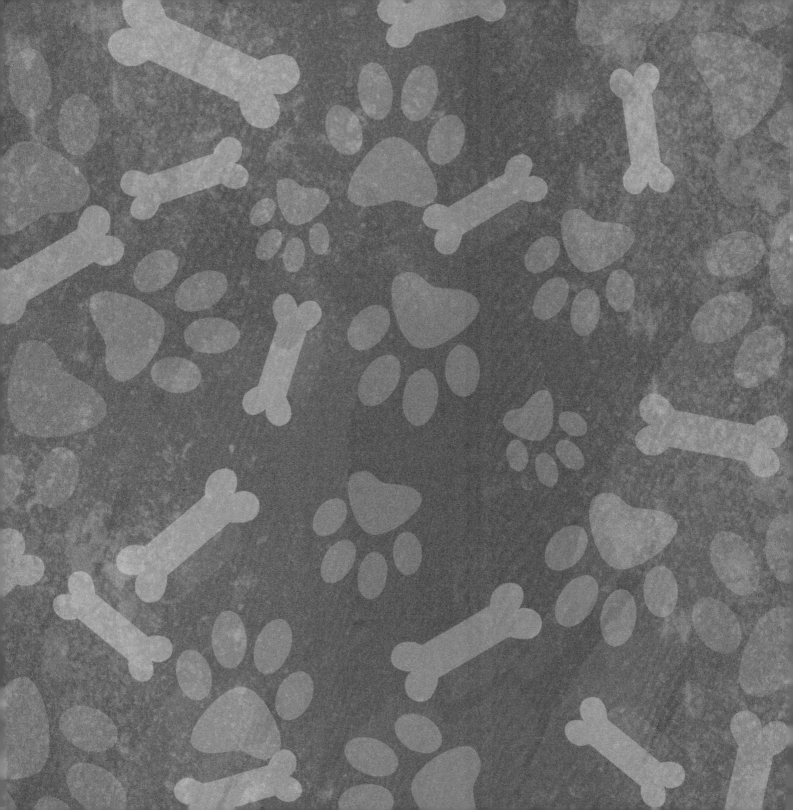

About the Story

This story is about friendship and a cow who didn't know how to be a friend and so she bullied the animals in the barnyard.

She watched from afar as the other animals sang, danced, told jokes, and laughed together. Beulah didn't know how to do those things. Secretly, she wanted to, but .... she didn't know how to be a friend.

She wasn't like a donkey who could play guitar or a butterfly who was certain she could sing. A flamingo who could weather a hurricane.

Beulah wasn't talented or brave or even able to play baseball.

Then one day, her life changed.

Popeye skips along the path to the barnyard.

The sun is shining.

There's a light breeze.

He whistles a happy tune.

Maybe there will be a new adventure today.

But, something is wrong!

Meeting Beulah

As Popeye arrives at the gate to the pasture, he runs into Beulah.

"Hi. I'm Popeye"

"So what?" she answers.

"Nice to meet you, Beulah."

"You know my name?"

"Sure. It's my business to know who is new in the neighborhood. I'm the official welcome-to-the-barnyard-guy. I'm a regular around here. You may have heard of me."

"Nope, never heard of you shrimp."

"Would you like to play or sing or race or tell jokes?" asks Popeye.

"You have to be kidding. Why would I want to do any of those things with you? You're a nerd and a loser; and, you're foolish," says Beulah.

"And you're a bully."

"No I'm not. I'm a cow."

"You're wasting my time. I bet you don't have a cell phone, credit cards, or even the internet. Get lost, loser."

Popeye is very sad. Why does Beulah hate him so much? All Popeye's friends can see he is sad, so they come over to find out what the problem is.

"This isn't like you, Popeye."

"Beulah said I'm a nerd, a loser, and foolish," says Popeye.

"Yeah. Her vocabulary isn't very good."

"A cow with an attitude."

"What did you do to make her angry?"

"She's not angry. She's a bully," says Popeye.

"What's a bully?"

Popeye thinks for a minute and then says, "How can I say this right? She thinks she is better than all of us so she makes fun of us."

"Why?"

"Dunno," Popeye says sadly.

The Barnyard Gang

"What's your name? What kind of animal are you?"

"I'm a llama and my name is Jose'. I come from Peru, and I speak Spanish. *Comprende?* I have been trained to ~~carry stuff on~~ my strong back."

"Stuff?"

"Yeah, stuff." says José.

"I've have never heard of a llama. You must be weird. You look weird. Where's Peru?"

"Ask Popeye. He's better with directions."

"Who?"

"Hi, I'm Cecil, and I'm a donkey."

"What kind of name is that? What do people call you?"

"Cecil. I'm from far away, just like Jose'. But, I'm from England. It's on the other side of the ocean."

"What's that on your head?"

"A bowler. We all wear them in jolly 'ol England."

"Bowler. Isn't that someone tossing a ball down an alley to knock down pins?"

"It's a traditional hat in my country. Wait 'til you see my top hat."

"Can't wait."

"Hi! I'm Porker. I've been waiting to meet you and welcome you to the barnyard."

"Why? Oh, forget it. Why's your name Porker?"

"What a silly question. Don't you know anything about pigs?"

"No. Can't really say I do. Why do you wear glasses?"

"So I can see."

"At last! One I recognize. You're a rooster."

"Right, Ms. Know-It-All. I have all these fancy feathers so I strut around the barnyard."

"Why do you do that?"

"What a silly question."

"Sounded like a good question to me. Name?"

"Dude."

"Zowie! What are you? What's your name?"

"I'm a flamingo, and my name is Gorgeous."

"You have to be kidding. How did you get a name like that?"

"Duh! Just look at me. Obvious."

"What are you doing here?"

"I didn't follow the crowd. I was trapped in a hurricane, and it dropped me here. I like it here. We play games and tell jokes and dance."

"What kind of animal are you"?

"My name is Olivia. I'm a butterfly."

"Why did you come here?"

"I wanted to join the Sunshines. It's a singing group. They may need a third singer. Maybe I can be the one."

"Butterflies don't sing."

"If you listen closely and believe, you can hear the song from the fluttering of my wings."

Baseball

Friends have been invited from the next field to play baseball.

Popeye is the outfielder.

Jose' is the catcher.

Farmer Hayseed is the umpire.

Gorgeous takes the microphone to announce the play-by- play action.

Kangaroo is up to bat. It's a homer!

Then there is a base hit from Tiger. Grizzly Bear makes it a triple.

The barnyard gang gets whomped. The other team wins.

"You won fair and square. Next week, OK?"

"You bet. Wouldn't miss it. You may want to work on that pitching arm, though. Just a thought."

Beulah has been hiding in the trees, reading the newspaper.

"I don't care", she says to herself.

She prances back to her stall in the barn, happy that she has made fun of those foolish animals.

"I'm smart and beautiful, and they're dumb and silly."

Trouble in the Back Pasture

Everything is calm in the barnyard until one day the animals hear,
"Moooooooo! Help!"
"It's coming from the back pasture."
"Do you think Beulah could be in trouble?"
"Pack your gear. We're off to the rescue."
"She's trapped in the barbed wire fence. Get your nail clippers!"
"I'll put a plan together. Come on, Cecil and Jose'. You're my main men."

Gorgeous sings soothing songs to Beulah and tells her how beautiful she is.

Popeye reads to her from his favorite book.

Dude dances and spreads his feathers to entertain her.

Porker tells her jokes.

Olivia does flips in the air. "Pretty cool, huh?"

Cecil is in the front.

José is in the back.

Dude is in charge of pulling away the wire.

"Yikes! This is hard work, but don't worry. I'm on the job. One, two, three - pull."

"I'm Free! I'm Free!"

"Thanks, guys and gals, and especially Popeye. You're quite a guy, Popeye. You and your friends could have let me stay in trouble. But you didn't."

"Popeye, I'm sorry I was so mean to you and your friends."

Farmer Hayseed gives treats to everyone, and they settle down together in the barnyard. Then, all the animals fall asleep right there in the barnyard, side by side, even Beulah. Beulah smiles in her sleep. She is dreaming of her barnyard friends. Yes, friends. Those special animals who helped her without her even asking.

That's just what friends do.

"Good night, Beulah."

"Good night, Popeye."

The end

This page is special. It's for you to color any way you want.

Dedications

To Kay, Myrna, Marilyn, and Laura,

my four pals from our school days in our small village. We all graduated from high school together, and three of us were even in kindergarten together.

We live in places far away from each other now but we share what's happening in our lives. We even manage to get together from time to time. They have been my constant supporters, reviewers, and critics.

Thanks, gals.
Betts

As my beloved Abuelito dedicated his book to his wife, my Abuelita, and family:

For my husband and for my whole family; for your support, comfort, help and devotion. For those whom I deprived of my usefulness and time in the process of creating of this book.
Holland

About the Author and Illustrator

The world is battling COVID-19, so Betts stays close to home. Olivia, her Aussie-doodle, is always at her side. She must have at least one canine. She sits on her patio with plants and flowers surrounding her. She's an avid gardener when she's not writing. She thinks of friends from near and far. Her life has been enriched by friendships.

Also by the author
"*I'm, Popeye and I'm a Very Special Dog*". A story of hope.

Holland specializes in children's illustrations. She received her bachelor of arts degree in Tennessee. She has been published in magazines, had a solo exhibition and illustrated a book. She lives in Franklin, Tennessee, with her beloved husband, three daughters and two dogs.

Friends

make the sun shine,
the stars twinkle,
and the flowers bloom,
and they put a song in your heart.

A donation is made to The Humane Society of Polk County for each book sold

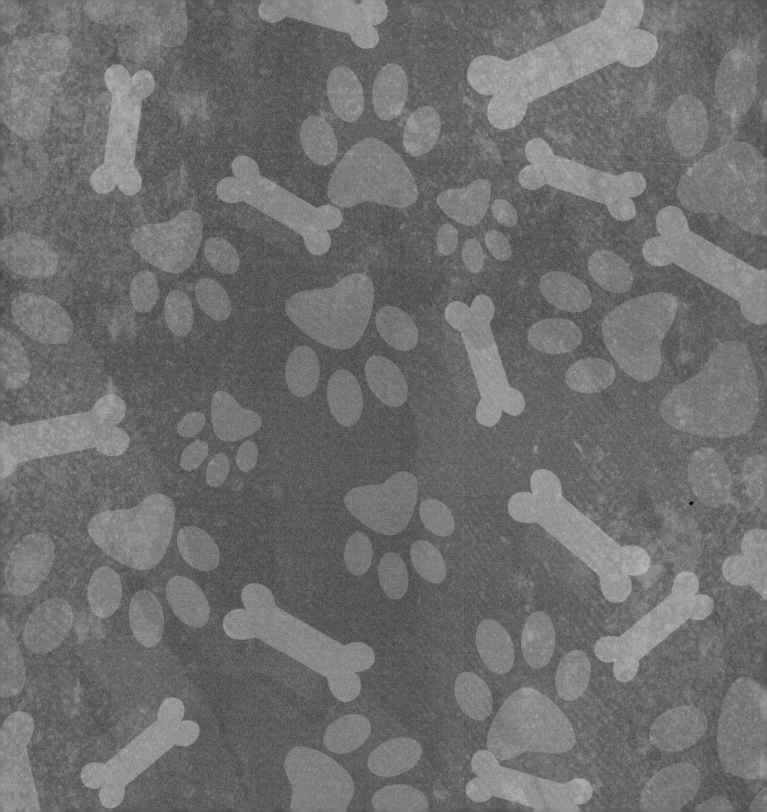